The Healing Power Within

HOW TO TAP THE INFINITE POTENTIAL
WITHIN YOURSELF

Ann Wigmore

AVERY PUBLISHING GROUP INC.
Wayne, New Jersey

The medical and health procedures in this book are based on the training, personal experiences, and research of the author. Because each person and situation is unique, the author and publisher urge the reader to check with a qualified health professional before using any procedure where there is any question as to its appropriateness.

The publisher does not advocate the use of any particular diet and exercise program, but believes the information presented in this book should be available to the public.

Because there is always some risk involved, the author and publisher are not responsible for any adverse effects or consequences resulting from the use of any of the suggestions, preparations, or procedures in this book. Please do not use the book if you are unwilling to assume the risk. Feel free to consult a physician or other qualified health professional. It is a sign of wisdom, not cowardice, to seek a second or third opinion.

Photo credit: Photographs by Frank Massa, Jr.

ISBN 0-89529-228-9

Printed in the United States of America

CONTENTS

4. The Fourth Dimensional Law of Love

5. The Human Aura

6. Meditation

7. Living Food Nourishment

FOREWORD

Ann Wigmore, founder of Hippocrates Health Institute, has received international acclaim during the past thirty years for her successful work with cancer, leukemia, arthritis, diabetes and other prevalent debilitating diseases. Through her extensive research and practical application of a nutritional approach to health problems, Ann Wigmore has demonstrated repeatedly that the body, given the opportunity, will heal itself.

Many books by Ann Wigmore have been published and read from Boston to Bombay on the subject of nutrition and the healing and rejuvenation of the body. This present book is her first to focus primarily on the spiritual aspect of humankind and on the healing and restoration of the spirit. This is not an unfamiliar subject to Ann Wigmore. Not only was spirituality her formal education as a young adult, but Ann has been living and practicing expanded consciousness in conjunction with her nutritional health program for most of her adult life.

The disclosures by Ann Wigmore presented here are not new principles. They are as old as the universe. In fact, they have been the underlying force and creative flow of the universe and all life since the beginning. These same principles that, when understood and used properly, can create an entire universe or a tiny complex organism are available to you to create anything you wish in your life on every level: spiritual, emotional, intellectual, material.

It is Ann's purpose in this book to reveal these rudiments to you in a simple straight forward manner so that you may begin today to employ an endless source of power that will allow you to manifest absolutely whatever you want in your life. What has taken her over seventy years to compile and understand fully, Ann now is offering to you and to everyone so that you will be able to start immediately on the road to abundance and prosperity in every aspect of your life. By the time you finish reading this handbook, you will have the tools to secure total personal freedom, unlimited happiness and success, perpetual youth and vitality, and very literally anything your heart desires.

The following pages contain a basic, practical disclosure of the process of heightened consciousness and lightened physiology. It is on this expanded level that human beings are able to allow whatever they want to be manifested in their lives. This power has always been with us and is as natural to us as it is for healthy lungs to breathe or healthy eyes to see. But much like disease can interrupt the natural, effortless functioning of an organ, so too can *dis ease* interrupt the natural, effortless functioning of the total Self. The power is still available to a blocked consciousness, such as air is still available to a collapsed lung, but it simply is not being utilized.

The difference between a lung and a person is choice. A person — even in a blocked state — can choose. And given an opportunity, given the information on how to tap the Life Force which is natural to all of us — which, in fact, is within each of us — *anyone* can choose and do *anything*. Herein, Ann Wigmore wishes to share that information, pass on the opportunity.

Connor Lourd

INTRODUCTION

In our world today things are happening and changing at an increasingly quickening pace. The energy vibrations influencing all life and growth on this planet are accelerating so steadily that we now must develop a new awareness of these forces. We need to develop a higher level of consciousness and a lighter physiology in order to expand and exist in this period of transition. The New Age is here — it is one of the greatest happenings that has come to the planet earth. It is the time when humankind is taking a giant step in our millions of years of evolution from "the cave" through "the village" through "the nation" into becoming planetary people. Our old securities are vanishing, and most of the established standards are being replaced as outdated habits and ideas are being discarded. A new vision of universal oneness is permeating the human spirit as the higher Self has begun its ascent to fulfill our destiny of freedom, love and total independence in body, mind and spirit. The infinite abundance of happiness and prosperity which is our birthright now can be ours for the asking. It will take nothing more than our awareness and acceptence. The time is here in human history for a heightened understanding and conformity to the laws of Nature so that we may reclaim our lost estate.

The cosmic law is — and always has been — in effect whether we choose to go with it or against it. To the degree in which we go with this one Force, freeing ourselves from petty programming and inappropriate preconceptions, actual miracles will manifest themselves in our lives. This unlimited freedom and power springs directly from our willingness to cooperate with the one Life Force of which we are a part. The Force, in fact, is within each of us. It is with this knowledge that we now are realizing that life has unending adventures as never before and a dynamic potential for total happiness and fulfillment on a consistent basis.

Why, then, has it been apparent in human history that people have not accepted and utilized this simple truth? Somewhere along the way human beings lost sight of the Natural law and, through that process, relinquished much of its limitless benefits. Humans lost the understanding or awareness and, as a result, deprived themselves of the endless supply of vitality, joy and prosperity that universal Energy constantly is offering to us. In the aftermath of this forgotten knowledge, many sociological institutions such as churches, philosophies and schools unwittingly perpetuated the obscurity throughout the Ages. A new re-educating currently is proceeding to rekindle the divine Spark within every human so that each one may tap the ultimate power of the Self — the link with the Life Force inherent in us. Our innate instinct for this, our natural power — suppressed, but never totally obliterated — is being released and expressed in the New Age. New Truth, new Energy, new Love and Light are being rediscovered by us the creatures of a wonderful resource of great wealth on all levels.

The success of our achieving our natural perfection in the New Age — and therefore peace, joy and prosperity for the world — depends upon the cultivation of a healthy life style: that is, accepting the freedom of the responsibility of self care in all phases of our lives. We now are assuming dominion over ourselves. This independence is effected through the letting go of inappropriate behavior and thought patterns that were a part of our early conditioning or programming. Any of the suffering of sickness, frustration, poverty or injustices in this abundant world is an unnecessary consequence of such patterning. When we replace these old obstructing patterns with a new method of constructive thoughts, we shall liberate the power of the creative Force in us. When we let go of all thoughts of lack or dependency and replace them with real thoughts of abundance and personal freedom, perpetual abundance and freedom will be manifested in our lives. Every thought has the power to bring into being the visible from the invisible. It is absolutely necessary for us all to understand that *everything we think, say or do comes back to us*. Every thought, word or action — without exception — manifests itself as an actual reality. In order to experience fullness and plenty in our reality, we must change our deficient thought patterns.

The accepting, the welcoming of change is a fundamental aspect of our ascent into joining with the universal living Energy. All of animate and inanimate nature responds automatically to the ever changing and expanding universe. Only humans have demonstrated resistance to growth in this way from era to era. This has resulted in the retardation of cosmic growth and perfection in our experience in the past. To the extent that we become maximally pliable, flexible and mobile, we shall experience total release and optimal growth. This process of opening up to higher consciousness and the bounty of Life can begin immediately, right now, today. You need only to choose and allow it into your life. It is right here in front of you, around you and within you awaiting your acceptance. Your personally allowing omnipotent Life Energy to flow freely through you is your step into the exciting new dimension of the Light and Harmony which is existing right now.

A great, seemingly sudden, burst of growth and unfoldment has become evident among humans during the past decade, the dawning of the New Age. Definite spiritual evolutionary developments are conspicuous in many human beings at this time. This spiritual evolution is paralled by the biological evolution of the etheric brain. It is this "light" brain that can allow unfoldment of the Self and expanded consciousness, because it functions on a higher vibrational plane. We can aid this biological transmutation to a higher vibration on a biochemical basis through living food nourishment. We also can aid our mental and spiritual transformation to a higher vibration through a conscious expansion of conciousness into the cosmic oneness of all life. With the understanding of personal unfoldment and knowing active participation in the law of Love — the very power of the one Force — the Aquarian Age will speed to fruition and each individual's potential will be realized.

Ann Wigmore

CHAPTER 1
"GOD", NATURE, AND US

From the viewpoint of the Absolute, time does not exist. Everything that *is* happening, *has* happened or *will* happen is happening all at once, a continuous *now*. Although our intuitive selves live in this ever present moment, on a linear level we experience time as a reality. The universe is known by us as being composed of relative realities (temporal) and absolute realities (eternal). Another common way of expressing this is: all is matter (relative reality) and all is energy (absolute reality). Matter is nothing but energy in a denser vibratory state. Matter and energy represent the two poles of the manifestation of the mind, matter being the denser and energy or spirit being the more subtle, alacrite and creative.

All the universe is a mental creation, and we and everything — though manifested in a visible, physical form — exist in the mind of the creative Force. This creative Force or Energy sometimes has been called "God"; but the concept of God is so vague and absurd for so many people that the term itself may have lost any of its original meaning. Words such as "God", "Prime Mover", "First Cause", "Supreme Goodness", "Creator" and so forth have been coined to describe the universal Substance/Energy which informs all life — which informs you — which, in fact, at your very center *is* you. And the instinctive human quest to find "God", to find the Ultimate, the Answer, is in reality the inborn desire for the human to connect with it Self. It is the human's natural desire to rejoin that natural center of awareness where all things are knowable and all things are possible. This journey is a surprisingly simple one, a far easier path to the absolute realization and power than any of the complex paradigms that have been concocted from misguided and misunderstood "truths". The path to your own Awareness is virtually effortless, because it simply is dealing in the natural, normal state of humans.

When we understand clearly that all is mind — that everything both visible and invisible springs from and exists in the one mind energy, the Universal Mind — we then are able to see that the entire universe with its planets, galaxies, suns and gods may be found in identical form within us. Everything positive emanates from the creative Energy which we, when we lift up our consciousness, readily can contact within ourselves. The apparant negative, "bad" or "evil" manifestations are merely unreal examples of undeveloped positive realities. In fact, in the ancient Essene language, the word "evil" literally means "nothing". It is important only to be tuned into the generating positive Life Force in order to avoid the disintegrating effects of the illusory undeveloped lower vibrations. Illusions, "lies" or anything else that creates chaos, pain, frustration, irritation, unhappiness or morbidity are misrepresentations of an unevolved, undeveloped life energy. "Badness" is merely undeveloped Good. "Wrong" is undeveloped Right. "Disease" is undeveloped Health. "Poverty" is undeveloped Wealth. "Misery" is undeveloped Bliss. "Fear" is undeveloped Peace. The negatives simply do not exist in real life.

Then how is it that we all have seemed to have experienced one or many of these distressing feelings and conditions at one time or another in our lives? These deteriorating manifestations gain "life" or come into existence as a direct result of our empowering them through a misguided use of the creative Energy within us. This is the consequence of our ignorance of the Law. Just as any thought, word or action that is cooperative with the infinite abundance of Nature can evince unlimited benefit in our lives, any negative action or thought on our part will bring adversity into our experience. To live consistently in a totally fulfilled state, materially, emotionally, mentally and spiritually, we must keep in continuous contact and movement with the *generating* force of Life. Whenever we lose sight of the real workings of this Energy, we unwittingly bring distress and disintegration into our lives. The first step, of course, is to *gain* sight of the totality of the Life Force — understand it — and then proceed from this understanding to move *with* it, unite with it. This is what is meant by cosmic consciousness.

The easiest way for us to contact the Universal Mind is through Nature and the laws of Nature. Nature is the manifestation of the Universal Mind in the earth: Abundance, creative Force, the vigorous Power of a fulfilled Life. And Nature is right here like the proverbial open book just waiting to be read. As the Tibetan masters repeatedly have said, the Truth is hidden for us all to see *right in front of our own eyes.*

Nature at all times is lavishing us with Abundance and watching over our welfare: but, when we break the Natural Law, we set ourselves against the Life Force. We destroy the Harmony of life within ourselves and encounter pain and misery. We punish and impoverish ourselves when we go against the Vitality and Abundance of Nature. The natural desire in the human is for prosperity, love and freedom — simply because *total* fulfillment is the birthright of the human being. When this fullness is not experienced in a personal life, or on a world wide basis, it is only because people have taken self defeating means in their quest for their fulfillment. Somewhere along the way they lost sight of the Law. The chapters immediately following deal with the laws of Nature.

CHAPTER 2
THE UNIVERSAL LAW OF ABUNDANCE

"There is one thing needful: everything,
The rest is vanity of vanities." G. K. Chesterton

There is no lack in the great universe.

The supply is unlimited, and there is NO restriction. All of the energy of the universe flows through us and demonstrates itself through our desires, thoughts and actions. And the greater our desires are, the greater amount of universal Energy will flow through us and demonstrate bigger and better things in our lives. The clue is not to ask in a miserly way — the key is to ask in a grand manner. This is true for everyone. A person with great material wealth and a huge amount of temporal power can — and should — ask for more, much more. A person starving and diseased can and should ask for more. And people who sometimes have good times and sometimes have bad times also can and most definitely should ask for *more.*

Each one of us on this planet earth must keep opening and opening until we have — or, *allow into our lives — nothing short of everything.* This is why we exist — and to fulfill this, our destiny, is our responsibility and our pleasure.

This opening of ourselves to receive the highest and best in our lives comes about by means of ridding the body and mind of degrading and depressing entities and filling the mind and body with the bounty and creative power of the Life Force, the Universal Spirit — *your* spirit. Your body is a manifestation of Life, the living Spirit, and so is your mind. The Living Spirit, the Universal Mind, is functioning in you at all times, even when your body and mind are obscuring Its fullness with dead food and deadening thought patterns. When your body is properly nourished and fully enlivened, and your mind is properly fed and completely opened, the totality of the Abundance of the Life force floods through you. Your inner Self becomes unshackled, and your ability to use all of the Power and Abundance of the One Force is released, because you have reunited with the Life Force — the real You.

The rejuvenation of your body and mind and the restoration of your unity with the abundance of the universe is accomplished by chasing out toxins and limitations with living food on both a carnal and mental basis. The more we living things ingest life, both bodily and spiritually, the more alive we become, and the more we can tap the Source of all Abundance which is *within ourselves.* We need not look anywhere else, because the cosmos is right here inside us, inside our bodies and minds. But since we all have accumulated a certain amount of deadening toxins both biologically and intellectually in our lives, our full cosmic power has been blocked, and our ability to experience all of its abundance has been restrained. These restrictions, which we have imposed on ourselves, can be irradicated by us. We are the ones who, unwittingly or not, have fastened the chains on our Selves, and it is we who can loose them.

Biologically, we can clean out any poisonous and dead material in our bodies and put in healthy, live substance by means of living food nourishment. And we can chase out any deadly and obstructing thought patterns mentally by consciously choosing only the best of everything and eliminating any deficiency, any lack. Your entering into complete Abundance and Power and perfect Happiness and Vitality need not happen overnight, although it certainly could — and, in fact, has in many cases in my experience. But whether your unfoldment occurs instantly, or whether it takes several days or several months, the point is that it *will* occur if you choose to let it happen. As soon as you decide to go with Nature's Law, to go with the Life Force, and then actively *do* go with It, your unfoldment automatically takes place; and all of your potential, the limitless Power of the universe, becomes actualized in you and for you.

Denials and Affirmations

On the mental or conscious plane, the method for bringing about your unfoldment to Universal Abundance and Prosperity is the intellectual process of Denial and Affirmation.

A denial is a declaration of rejection.

An affirmation is a declaration of acceptance.

A statement of denial is used to free oneself from lack, dependency and limitation; and a statement of affirmation is used to fill oneself with abundance, freedom and prosperity.

When a statement of denial is used, it always should be followed with a statement of affirmation. Affirmations may be used by themselves.

For example, to let Universal Abundance into your life, declare:

"There is no lack in the great universe, and there is no lack in me (statement of denial). I now choose and accept all of the abundance and prosperity of the great universe which I now know has always been mine (statement of affirmation)."

You may use the statement of affirmation by itself. Declare:

"I now choose and accept all of the abundance and prosperity of the great universe which I now know has always been mine."

The statement of denial rejects — casts out — restrictive, limiting, inappropriate thought patterns; and the statement of affirmation accepts — puts in — appropriate, real, abundant thought patterns that can manifest anything and everything you need or want in your life. It is because the affirmation is the vehicle of the manifestation that it can be used without a denial. A denial, though, is a powerful "cleaner" and can create room in your consciousness or mind for the affirmation to settle in and take hold. If you had a pail of dirty water and kept pouring pure water into it, eventually the clear water would replace the cloudy water in the pail, and the pail would be filled with pure water only. But if you empty the pail and clean it out and pour the fresh water into it, there will be more room in the pail for the good water to fill right then. In a similar manner, denials make room for affirmations in the mind. So use denials if you feel you need them when you think they will help your affirmations — but remember it is the affirmation that is the effective statement.

It is important to understand that the efficacy of the method of denial and affirmation relates directly to the conviction you put into your declarations. When you are convinced of your own statements, your own words, it is then on the mental level that you convince yourself of the truth and reality that they bear. Therefore, *do not be meek* with your declarations — *Command, Demand, Call our in a loud voice.*

Many people have broken right through restrictions that were blocking their innate power the very first time that they made an affirmation or denial and affirmation. They did not only *believe* — they *knew, felt* and *desired* what they were saying, and they evoked the manifestation instantly. They had conviction in their statements. They convinced their minds with their spoken word.

The reason why your mind has to be convinced is because it is that part of you — the mind or ego — that stands at the threshold between You and the Life Force. It is your mind, your ego, your consciousness that can be conditioned or programmed for oppression or prosperity (or anything else, for that matter). Since the mind is a mental entity, it is programmed or conditioned by intellectual input such as thoughts or words or ideas. What is said to it, and what it *accepts* of what is said to it, determines how much of the Life Force it allows your inner Self to rejoin. And the more of the power of the Universal Life Force that your mind accepts and allows into You, the more of Its energy will be in your command in your experience and in your life. It is, therefore, absolutely necessary to impress your mind of this fact.

Your affirmations may be general, or they may be specific to an immediate need.

Should you need some specific thing or attribute at any particular time, you may affirm:

> "I now choose and accept the perfect
> ____________from the life force which is
> (Name it)
> within me, in a perfect way."

The general affirmation would be:

> "I now choose and accept all of the

perfect power and abundance of the life force which is within me and every thing in the universe."

The general affirmation includes the specific affirmation, because the general affirmation is a totality. But if you feel the need to focus on a specific item or desire, the specific affirmation will be thoroughly effective. *Any affirmation declared properly, with conviction, will manifest that which it affirms.* It is best, however, to use general affirmations even while you are affirming specific needs, because general affirmations impress your mind with the *totality* of the abundance of the Life Force. You could short change yourself (and everyone else) if your mind or consciousness is not yet completely opened to the Totality. That is to say, you might be manifesting cents when you just as easily could be manifesting dollars, shoes when you could be manifesting feet, something when you could be manifesting everything.

Use specific affirmations when you think they are necessary, but always keep impressing your mind with general or universal affirmations of Abundance and Energy until your mind finally opens enough to accept it all.

Whether or not you think your affirmations are getting to your mind, they are. And, if it take repetition to impress your mind of your affirmations, then give your mind the repetition it requires — shout your affirmations to your mind twenty four hours a day: say them right OUT LOUD when you are alone with yourself, THINK them during the day when you do not declare them aloud, and dream them while you sleep. Your mind will catch on. And the moment it does, your mind, your ego, your consciousness — that part of you standing at the threshold between the Life Force and your inner Self — will open up and open the gate for your inner Consciousness to merge with your super Consciousness, the Life Force, and all will be actualized.

You see, it is your inner Consciousness that is the part of you that is the Life Force, and it is your super Consciousness that is the Life Force, and it is your consciousness, your mind, that is not the Life Force, but rather, the mediator between the Life Force of the inner and super Consciousness. And that is why your consciousness must be opened — it must expand — to let the Life Force reunite with Itself in your inner Self. It is imperative, therefore, on a mental level that you impress your mind with the absolute reality of the Abundance, Prosperity and Power of the Life Force.

There may be times in your day to day life during your progress toward complete unfoldment and enlightenment that you find yourself falling into old patterns of depression and frustration. At these times, affirmations of the Life Force may seem remote to you — they may, in fact, seem superficial and even annoying to you. These are possibly the most important times for you to affirm and affirm and - *affirm*. You may not feel the effect of your affirmations at all during these times, at least in the beginning, but *keep on affirming*. Your affirmations will be working unbeknownst to you until finally, your mood will relax and your perspective will broaden and suddenly you will be back with the flow of Life and Its abundance. The limitations of any earlier petty programming will be lifted from your consciousness through this process, and you will be set free to continue your advance to your total unfoldment and complete union with the limitless power of the Life Force.

Another peculiar occurrence I have noted during my years of experience in this field both in myself and in others is that past obstructing moods and thought patterns tend to come out stronger than ever just at the moment that they are about to be cast out your consciousness permanently. It is very much like what is known medically as a "healing crisis" — but in this case on a spiritual level.

A healing crisis occurs biologically in an organism when its cells and tissues are being thoroughly cleansed of old wastes and toxins that the organism has accumulated through improper nourishment, environmental factors and any past diseases it may have encountered. Many of my guests at Hippocrates Health Institute, for example, actually exhibit symptoms of a past illness or even the effects of a "bad apple" (so to speak) which they may have ingested years ago while they are cleansing and rebuilding their bodies through the process of detoxification and rejuvenation of their cells. The healing crisis will occur even if they are "healthy" (that is to say, even if they have no apparant "disease" at the time), because the cellular debris from past disease or improper nourishment embedded in their bodies must rise to the surface to be expelled and replaced with healthy, living tissue.

The same kind of phenomenon seems to occur in the purging and final expanding of consciousness. As I say, you may feel the most discouraged just before the *final* opening of your ego takes place, but it is crucial at that moment to LET GO: *relax, affirm* and let all of the negativity formerly impressed upon your mind *go for good.*

There are a number of affirmations presented in the appendix of this book: however, you may compose your own as well. It is important only that they are worded properly.

Phrasing Affirmations Correctly

1. ***Always use the present tense, not the future.*** Do not say, "I shall have . . ."; say, "I have . . .". The reason for this is, as we have said earlier, everything already exists on the mental plane in the Universal Mind. It is the function of an affirmation to manifest the visible from the invisible.

2. ***Always use a positive statement.*** Do not say, "I am not sick", for example: say, "I am healthy." (As mentioned earlier in the chapter, if you feel the need to use a denial to make way for your affirmation, follow it immediately with the affirmation, e.g., "I am not sick. I am healthy.")

3. ***Always use absolute conviction, feeling, intensity and concentration.*** Do not mumble or merely rattle off your affirmations. If even for the moment, put all of your strength and desire

into what you are affirming. When you put ALL of the power of concentration of ALL of your mind into an affirmation, it manifests INSTANTLY.

4. ***Always affirm perfection, abundance and increase.*** Make sure you do not limit the Totality of the Life Force in your declarations, even when you are making a specific affirmation. Use words such as "all, "abounding", "perfect", etc . . .

The Universal Mind, The Life Force, already has all the Abundance, Bounty and Bliss which has always been yours created for you in a perfect way on the invisible plane. The only thing you need to do is to allow it to manifest visibly in your life — It *is* your Life.

CHAPTER 3

THE MAGNETIC LAW OF CAUSE AND EFFECT

"You must have done something, Kate."
Robert Galbraith

Everything attracts what it radiates.

Everything effects that which it causes. Anything causes that which it effects. Nothing happens by chance. YOU cause what you effect. You are the one who has caused every single thing that has come into your life. YOU radiate what you attract. It is you who have brought into your life every situation or incident in your experience. Nothing comes to you by "accident". Everything that happens to you is a direct result of what you have put forth.

The universe is made of radiant energy flowing through magnetic fields. Our thoughts, words, actions — our very beings — are made of this radiant energy that attracts to itself that which it radiates. Whatever you think, feel, say, do or are comes back to you without exception.

Like all of Nature's laws, the cosmic law of Cause and Effect is always in force whether people are aware of it or not. When you do become aware of this law and how it functions, you can employ it for your maximum benefit (and, consequently, the benefit of the world). Everything in Nature works along definite, logical lines according to principles. These forces will work for anyone who has the key of understanding.

To understand the law of Cause and Effect, you need only to understand fully that *everything comes to you from within yourself.* There is nothing outside ourselves that creates anything that comes to us. We create everything that comes to us by means of the vibrations of our ideas, thoughts, feelings, words and actions. In other words, we create our own lives. And the higher you allow your mental vibrations to be, the more expansive your creative ability becomes, because you are liberating the inner Consciousness which is one with the creative Force of the universe. No human being has any more power than any other. It is that simple. The Universal Mind which creates absolutely everything plays no favorites. The great people of the world were not "super" beings — they possessed exactly the same ability as we do, but they learned to draw upon their inner Consciousness.

Thomas Edison said, "Our mind is like the wireless operator. It uses right or wrong thought currents. If we are not in tune with the infinite or to higher vibrations, failure is the result." It is just as easy to think in terms of abundance and health as it is to think in terms of limitation and sickness, but we need to raise our rate of vibration through the understanding of the cosmic law of Cause and Effect. We then can release the inner Consciousness to flow with this principle, thereby keeping us in tune with the infinite, the higher vibrations, and we can actively and knowingly create our lives as we want them to be.

Visualization

In addition to the method of *Affirmation,* one can engage the laws of Nature on the conscious level through the method of *Visualization.* Visualization is the intellectual process by which you manifest something you want by imaging it, imagining it. It could be a situation, a goal, an object, a characteristic — anything. There is no limitation in Creation. In visualization, one pictures — *sees* — in the imagination what one wishes to manifest. It is the way to bring the visible into being from the invisible through images in the "mind's eye". Affirmations are verbal; visualizations are pictorial. Affirmations manifest what is affirmed by means of declarations; visualizations manifest what is visualized by means of images or mental pictures. Affirmation and visualization may be used together; in fact, they will potentiate the effect of each other when they are employed accurately.

How to Visualize

It is important first to relax deeply and to enter into a quiet meditative state. This is what is known as "going into the silence". In deep relaxation, the brain wave actually changes and becomes slower. This is called the ALPHA level. The more active BETA level is the brain wave usually at work during our busy waking activities during the day. We experience the more creative ALPHA level just before sleep and just upon waking and during periods of meditation or deep relaxation. It is the ALPHA pattern that, on a brain wave basis, allows you to contact your inner Self, the Life Force, that part of you which is part of Infinite Intelligence. The process of change into expanded consciousness does not occur on superficial levels through mere "positive thinking". Your inner transformation into your natural union with Universal Energy requires your contacting your inner or higher Self. It is on this deeper, or, more precisely, *real* level that the blocks to your unfoldment are released and your power of manifestation set free.

If you already have your own method of entering into deep relaxation or a meditative state or the ALPHA level, by all means use that method if you feel comfortable with it. If you never as yet have "gone into the silence" consciously, the following simple method will be thoroughly effective:

1. ***Sit comfortably with your spine straight, balanced and relaxed.*** This posture permits energy to flow evenly through you without interruption.

You may sit on a chair or cross-legged on the edge of a pillow on the floor, whichever is more comfortable for you. Just make sure that your back is vertical and balanced and that you are very comfortable.

It is helpful to face North or East (because of the electro-magnetic currents of the planet), and also to be in a dark, quiet room if you can arrange it, at least initially. (Very soon you will find you will be able to enter into a meditative state anywhere and anytime you want.)

2. ***Close your eyes and breathe slowly and deeply, inhaling and exhaling fully.*** Let your inhalations and exhalations take six or more seconds each, but don't time yourself. Let this slow, deep, even respiration come naturally from your inner bodily rhythm. While doing this, concentrate only on your breath, letting everything else in your mind go, and you will go right into the meditative state of deep relaxation.

3. ***Relax each muscle of your body one by one.*** Relax your toes, feet, ankles, calves, knees, thighs, pelvis, fingers, forearms, elbows, waist, upperarms, thorax, shoulders, neck, jaws, tongue, lips, cheeks, ears, nose, eyes, eyebrows, forehead, scalp . . .

4. ***Slowly count down from ten to one.*** Go deeper and deeper and relax more and more with every count. By the count of one, you will be in a deep, calm, quiet state of mind.

5. ***Imagine energy flowing up from the earth through you into the cosmos and imagine energy flowing down from the cosmos through you into the earth.***

Imagine and *feel* the energy from the center of the earth where you are sitting flowing up through your spine and body going gently out through the top of your head.

Imagine and *feel* energy from the universe flowing into the top of your head down through your body to the center of the earth where you are sitting.

As you consciously allow the earth energy to flow up through you into the cosmos and the cosmic energy to flow down through you into the earth, you are achieving a balance of energy which opens your Self and increases your power of manifestation.

You are now ready to visualize:

1. ***Imagine something you wish to manifest.*** It can be anything you want: an object, a relationship, a business deal, a financial gain, an increase in health, a spiritual quality — anything at all that you want, need or desire.

Picture or feel it clearly. Don't force it — simply allow it to flow into your imagination. Let it have as many details as you like to make it real.

If negative thoughts or feelings come into your mind, don't entertain them, don't repress them. Just let them go by and keep your focus on the beautiful, bountiful, blissful scene of your visualization.

Feel it, *Sense* it, and, above all, *Desire* it from the very center of your being with all your heart.

2. ***Imagine the scene as already existing in a perfect way.*** Don't limit yourself — there is no limit in the great universe. Imagine the highest and best expression of the thing you want to manifest in your visualization.

Imagine it as happening right now. To be successful with the method of visualization, you must visualize your desire as already existing. This is because it already really *does* exist in the Universal Mind. And the function of the visualization is to draw on that universal mind Energy to manifest the visible from the invisible.

3. ***Surround your visualization with a sphere of radiant light and let it go.*** When you clearly have felt, sensed and experienced your visualization as vividly as you possibly can, with all the desire that is in you (*but without force or attachment*), surround it with a great sphere of radiant light. Let this great sphere of radiant light containing your visualization float happily up into the cosmos where it will attract the appropriate energies of the universe to manifest the visualization.

Now you may come out of the meditative state, feeling both relaxed and energized. Take a few deep breaths and open your eyes. Stretch your limbs, head and torso slowly, get up easily, and return to your usual activity.

That is all there is to it. Your visualization may manifest immediately or very quickly or sometime later. Even if your visualization does not manifest instantly, the process of its eventual manifestation will have begun with your very first visualization. The energy has been put out, and it cannot fail to manifest. It is the law of Cause and Effect. This does not mean that you cannot repeat your visualizations. In fact, I have noted that, in most cases when a visualization does not manifest immediately, repetition of the visualization is quite helpful to keep one's energy focused on the desire or the goal. This repetition seems to accelerate the energy or vibration of the manifestation which is already in progress to its completion.

When to Visualize

It is best to set aside certain times each day for your periods of visualization. The best times for these sessions usually are right after you awake, just before you go to sleep, and some time about midway in your waking hours. It is not necessary to devote more than fifteen minutes to your visualization periods, but you may make them longer or shorter according to what feels comfortable or complete to you in any given session of visualization. As you grow more accustomed to visualizing — which, by the way, will happen in a very short time — you will find that visualization will become second nature to you. You will find that you will be visualizing — or at least focusing energy toward your visualizations — more and more throughout the day, even when you are not in your meditative visualization sessions. This simply means that, as visualization becomes more common to you, you will find that you will be able to focus on the object of your meditative visualizations anytime you wish, even as you go about your daily activities or concerns.

Affirmation and Visualization

You can increase the energy of your visualizations with affirmations. During your meditative visualization sessions (and also throughout the day) affirm that your desire or goal already exists, that it is happening *right now*. Speak to it and to yourself (aloud or silently) in positive, encouraging and convinced statements. Give thanks that it already exists. This will impress your consciousness with the fact that it already really DOES exist. And the moment your consciousness KNOWS and ACCEPTS your visualization, the visualization will manifest, and usually in a very short time. Your visualization will manifest instantly when you *truly Desire the object of the visualization, absolutely KNOW that it exists, and are completely willing to* ***ACCEPT*** it.

The method of visualization is another way in which we can unblock the barriers which we ourselves have set against the abundance and supply of the Life Force. It is a way in which we can allign ourselves with the manifesting power of the universe and use this Natural energy to create our own lives. With this understanding, you can consciously and consistently employ the natural law of Cause and Effect for your limitless good. You are able right now to experience all of the Abundance and creative Energy of the Life Force. The only thing needed for your part was to know about it, and the only thing needed from your part is to go with it and experience it.

What a joy it was when I first discovered that changing my thought patterns really worked in my life by allowing me to have happiness and positive experiences. This new awareness, coupled with the understanding of why I had my particular physical problems and how I had unknowingly created them made a great difference in my life. Now I could stop blaming life and other people for what was wrong and could, for the first time, take full responsibility for my own experiences. Without either reproaching myself or feeling guilty, I could see how to avoid new future thought patterns of disease and limiting conditions and how to create health and abundance.

What we really are is Life, Love, Wisdom, Peace, Power, Beauty and Joy. Anything different is something that has entered into our thinking and has been placed in the conscious mind where it is acted upon under the law of Cause and Effect. Our thoughts, past and present, manifest in our conduct and relationships with others whom we contact and with ourselves. With the understanding of the Natural law, we begin to work toward our *true* characteristics.

CHAPTER 4

THE FOURTH DIMENSIONAL LAW OF LOVE

"It knows about it all — It knows — It knows." Omar Khayyam

Love is the Life Force in manifestation.

Love manifests the Life Force instantly. It is the strongest radiant magnetic force in the universe. Love is the instant link between you and the Life Force. It is the expression and power of your inner Self, your higher Self, the Life Force Itself. In Love, there is no need of rational processes to expand the conscious mind. Love transcends the consciousness, or, better, splits it wide open into full awareness of and union with the Totality. Love is not intellectual, it is intuitive. It knows better — that is, it KNOWS.

Pure love pours itself out and draws the same to itself instantly, synchronistically — it does not need to seek or demand. Love is a cosmic phenomenon that opens the human to the fourth dimension where all things are possible, where all things are knowable, where all things exist. It is in the fourth dimensional world of awareness that we can see, experience and know all things and ideas in their real and perfect completion, in their actual existence.

Love transcends duality or the belief in duality. In reality there is only Oneness, and Love is the ultimate experience of Reality. Love prospers, creates, increases, attracts and enjoys. It is the fusion of you and the whole Energy and Substance of the Life Force. It is the fusion of you and all other parts or expressions of the Life Force. In Love, you and your Self and everyone else and their Selves and every single manifested fragment of the Whole comes together and becomes the one, simple, unfragmented Totality of the Life Force.

For your total unfoldment it is necessary that you be in Love. Love is not a tool for your unfoldment, Love *is* your unfoldment. Love is not a tool for success, Love *is* Success. Love is not a tool for prosperity, Love *is* Prosperity. Love is not a method of joy, Love *is* Joy. Love is not a step by step approach to the Life Force, Love *is* the Life Force. In fact, without Love, you will perish. All disease and all unhappiness, at the bottom line, is a result of violation of the law of Love.

You do not have to wait for Love to come to your from somewhere or some person or something. You take initiation in Love from *within*. As with Life, Abundance and Prosperity, Love already exists within you waiting to be released and sent out into the ethers and substance of the universe. When you send out real Love, real Love returns to you with all its benefits, power and joy. Real love is not fearful, is not jealous, is not anxious, is not grasping — in fact, it irradicates such barriers to fulfillment. When you allow real Love to pour out of You — whether on a personal basis to a particular object of your affection or on an impersonal basis to the world at large — it is necessary to let it go with an open hand and heart and mind. It is in this outgoing detached manner that perfect Love returns to you, and you will experience all the limitless favors of the Universal Love of the Life Force.

When you are in the state of Love, the intellectual methods for expanding your consciousness described in the preceding chapters no longer will be necessary to allign you with the power of the Life Force, because Love is intuitive rather than intellectual. It is the bee-line to the Life Force and allows you to live in the Life Force. When you let yourself open your Self to pure Love, everything else that you want or need will be added to you. It is as simple as that.

You, of course, may employ all the tools you now have in order to reach the state of Love where all things are actualized. In fact, it is advisable to use these consciousness expanding techniques to help you enter into the natural condition of Love. Affirm pure Love for yourself and others any time throughout the day and in your periods of meditation and visualization. In your periods of visualization, imagine and *feel* pure Love pouring out of you into the cosmos where it will unite with the One Energy of Universal Love. When you release real Love from your inner Self, you become one with the power of the creative and sustaining Life Force, Universal Love. There is no greater power in the universe.

Visioning

Visioning is the direct contact with the Life Force or Universal Energy through your inner or higher Self. Visualization is a *mental* process governed by the *reasoning* or *conscious* mind, whereas visioning is an *intuitive* process governed by the *super conscious* or *inner Self*. In visualization, you get a clear image of something, accept it, and allow it to manifest.

In *Visioning,* you get in touch with the Life Force through intuition, ask It what you want, and your goal, desire or destiny automatically comes into being. Because visioning is intuitive, it is not based on belief alone — it knows.

Intuition springs from the heart, or the energy field surrounding the heart. It is necessary to open up this energy field — to open up your heart — for visioning to take place. When the heart center is open, you feel truly loving, loved, safe and generous. You feel and really are connected with others, with nature, with the universe, instead of feeling separate, isolated, wary, or even hostile to the world outside. When we open the heart center, miracles suddenly start manifesting in our lives. The things for which we ask start rushing to us without our having to do anything else to bring them into our lives, because the energy that connects us with the Life Force is allowed to flow freely without interruption.

It is fear, worry, guilt and doubt that interrupts or stops the flow of this creative energy and thereby separates us from this Power. When the heart center is open, such negative, limiting, inappropriate entities are dissolved, and your untainted power of manifestation is released completely, because the opening of the heart center puts you directly in touch with your higher Self.

Opening the Heart Center

1. ***Sit with your spine straight, balanced and relaxed.*** You may sit in a chair with your feet flat on the floor, or on a pillow with your legs crossed. Face North or East.

Rest your hands on your knees with your palms open and facing up. Make sure you are very comfortable and that your clothing is very loose fitting. (In fact, if possible, don't wear any clothes at all during these sessions.)

2. ***Close your eyes and breathe deeply and easily.*** With each exhalation, allow all tension to flow gently out of you. With each inhalation, feel vital energy flow easily into you. Continue to breathe comfortably and easily.

3. ***Envision a many petalled flower bud made of radiant golden pink light within your heart.*** Allow the many petals of radiant golden pink light to open gently and expand. Feel the brilliant gentle golden pink light fill you with its warmth, love, strength and safety.

After a while, allow the petals of this brilliant golden pink light to unfold and expand more and more to surround you and the place where you are with its radiant glow.

Let this peaceful golden pink brilliance keep unfolding and expanding from your heart to surround the building or field or wherever it is that you are. Let this golden pink light continue to expand and extend as far as feels comfortable for you at this time. You may feel it continue to unfold to surround the town, the state, the country, the world, the universe. Just let it expand as far as it comfortably can in any session.

Feel the intense warmth, safety, strength and expansion of this friendly golden - pink radiance as you bathe in its glow.

You are now ready for visioning.

You are now in the visionary state.

You now experience your inner or higher Self in all its fullness and intuition and omniscience.

You now feel your superconsciousness filling you completely and pouring out of you and into you and all around you.

You do not *do* anything for this to happen, you do not *think* anything for this to happen, you do not *affirm* anything for this to happen, you do not *visualize* anything for this to happen.

With your heart center open, the complete release of your higher Self just simply happens all by itself — and instantaneously.

In this state, your inner Consciousness is in complete contact with the Life Force.

In this state, it is not your *rational* self that is allowing and accepting the manifestation of your affirmations and visualizations.

In this state, your needs and desires are manifesting through your *spiritual* Self.

Also, in this state, you know what your true needs and desires really are, with clear, unclouded vision.

And you also know that they all are being fulfilled *right now.*

Actually, the reason that we all feel the need to have certain *things* manifested in our lives is because of our more fundamental need to have our *lives themselves* manifested — and manifested to the fullest. When we are alligned with the law of Love, we experience the full manifestation of our lives in their natural perfection of growth and increase. When we are in accordance with the law of Love, our lives manifest perfectly, and all of the things that we want or need manifest automatically.

You undoubtedly have experienced certain times in your life when everything just seemed to work out effortlessly, even magically. During these times you may have felt so in tune or so peaceful or so wonderfully alive that everything just seemed to fall into place naturally. These were the times when you happened to have been spontaneously in harmony with the law of Love, when your inner Self popped out and prevailed and you were in open contact with the Life Force. With the understanding of the law of Love and through the use of visioning, you no longer have to wait for these random spurts of wholeness and fulfillment to occur in your life. You instead can be in constant touch with the Totality on a consistent basis. Your inner Consciousness can be set free and remain free to draw complete Life into your life *all of the time.*

I cannot repeat enough that all it takes is your *awareness* of this one positive force, your *understanding* of it, your having a simple effective method to *employ* this force, and your willingness to go ahead and experience It, use It, and enjoy ALL of Its benefits.

Giving and Receiving

Love is total acceptance without any expectation or limit. When we give out Love with no expectations of return, the Love within us expands, and as we give, we simultaneously receive. When we focus only on *giving*, inner Peace is released in us instantly. And when we focus on giving at every instant in our lives, we experience Peace, Joy and Love on a consistent basis.

Giving is the extending of our love with no conditions, no expectations and no boundaries. True giving does not try to change anyone or anything — it accepts everything *as it is*. When we live our lives giving or releasing Real Love from within, we live a life of perfect Abundance and Joy, because through giving we are constantly receiving Real Love which is the essence of the Life Force.

It is when our focus is on getting that conflict and distress enter into our lives, because the attitude of getting exists in linear time — that is, it is transient. Love and the releasing or giving of Love elevates us to the fourth dimension where we experience the eternal, the perpetual, the Real — where everything exists in its nautral state of unity and completion. Since Love does not project illusions, as can our egos when they are fearful or misguided, it allows us to accept direction from our inner, intuitive Selves, our true means of *knowing*. And with this intuitive direction comes the way of actualizing the direction, whether or not the way is immediately apparent.

It is important that you continue to understand that absolutely everything you need, you have *right now*, and that what we really are, essentially, is Love. In fact, Love is the only Reality. and through Love, you can draw upon anything and everything from the Life Force. Love is the Life Force in manifestation.

CHAPTER 5
THE HUMAN AURA

The human being is surrounded by energy fields that flow in, through and around the body. The forms of these energies range from simple electrical impulses to higher spiritual or vital forces, which are known collectively as the HUMAN AURA. This individual aura emanates from and surrounds each person. The aura is a force field of swirling frequencies in various colors that is readily and clearly perceivable to the clairvoyant. Recently, the human aura has been able to be photographed with the development of the Kirlian camera. You and everybody else very probably have sensed the aura of another from time to time, even if you did not actually see the rays of this force field vividly.

The rays of the human aura project from the physical, emotional and spiritual body and surround the human being from head to toe in an egg-shaped outline. The rays may extend outward as much as six feet at the widest point of the aura, which is around the area of your midsection. In addition to clairvoyants in our culture, people of other cultures in the worlds, such as the Tibetans, can see the human aura as easily as you can see the human body. You could be trained or train yourself to do likewise. It is merely a matter of education or exposure to the aura's existence.

As we have said, the rays of the aura emanate from both the physical and spiritual body and are indicative of the physical and spiritual condition of a person at any given time. The observation of the aura has been used for diagnosis in both spiritual and physical areas. For example, if the rays projecting from a particular organ of an individual appear muddied or brownish in color, this indicates a possible future degeneration of the tissues of that organ *before* it actually occurs in the physical body. Preventative measures, therefore, can be taken to prohibit the degeneration of the organ before it happens. The same holds true for the emotional, mental and spiritual condition of the individual. In fact, the emotional, mental, spiritual and physical bodies of each person are all interwoven and intereffect one another continuously. This is, of course, another reason for the necessity of balance in all of these areas for the health and wholeness of the individual.

The condition of our aura determines our susceptibility or non-susceptibility to all elements and vibrant influences. The more evolved one becomes through knowledge, training and experience, the less susceptible the aura is to the lower vibrations or contagions — both physical and spiritual; and the more the aura is in tune with the higher vibrations. This is why certain doctors or healers or anyone of higher evolution can walk "among the crowd" and not contract the lower level vibration of sickness. On the contrary, "the crowd" may experience the benefits issuing from the more highly developed aura of the more evolved person which can be healing emotionally, spiritually and physically.

The living body exists in a condition of perpetual change, and in order for the body to remain alive, it needs to be supplied constantly from three distinct sources: It needs (1) *food* for its digestion, (2) *air* for its breathing, and (3) *vitality* for its absorption. This *vitality* is an energetic force which exists at once in three forms, physiological, personal and spiritual, (the human body, the human soul, the human spirit).

The Seven Chakras

There are seven energy centers in the human emitting swirling auric rays that are the points of connection and continuation of the vitality force necessary to the life of the human. These energy centers or force centers are known as CHAKRAS. (The word "chakra" has entered into our vocabulary from Sanscrit and literally means "a wheel".) The chakras are swirling or rotating constantly and are constantly fed with the vital force of Universal Energy. They feed and interflow throughout your physiological, personal and spiritual bodies (that is to say, your body, soul and spirit as long as you are alive. In fact, your life is absolutely dependent on the continuous flow of energy through the chakras.

When less developed, the chakras appear as glowing dully. The more developed they become, the more blazing and brilliant they appear. They are in operation in every existing person to a greater or lesser degree as the body cannot exist without the energy flow in the chakras. In a less developed less evolved person, the chakras spin in a relatively sluggish motion, with possibly just enough movement to keep the life existing and no more. The more evolved or developed we become, the more our chakras glow and pulsate with more and more living light, and greater amounts of energy pass through them. With this increase of vital energy, the more our faculties open and unfold, and we are able to experience higher and more expanded conditions of life.

The Location and Description of the Seven Chakras

The seven chakras have become associated with certain parts of the physical body because of their location. Each chakra is of a predominant discernable color that is visible in its rays, and each chakra is associated with a certain aspect of your being.

1. *The Root Chakra* is located at the base of the spine. The color of its energy is fiery red which gives physical vitality. This center is associated with sexual and procreative energy which helps to rebuild the physical parts of the body and mind when it is flowing freely.

2. *The Spleen Chakra* is located in the small of your back about half way between the base of your spine and your navel. The color of its energy is bright orange which serves to specialize and disperse the vitality that comes from the sun. The energy of this center is

associated with feelings and emotions, and when flowing freely, helps to dissolve anger, resentment and confusion.

3. ***The Solar Plexus Chakra,*** which is also-called the *Navel* or *Umbilical Chakra*, is located behind the navel in the region of the solar plexus. The color of its energy is yellow which develops feelings and emotions into inspiration and ideas. The energy of this center is associated with the beginnings of intuitional guidance, and when flowing freely, initiates us into wisdom.

4. ***The Heart Chakra*** is located between your shoulder blades behind your heart. The color of its energy is brilliant green which develops intuition, growth and love. The energy of this center is associated with compassion, understanding and love, and when flowing freely, permits you to operate through intuition. It promotes your interconnection with life and your relationships with others.

5. ***The Throat Chakra*** is located just below your larynx or voice box at the base of your skull. The color of its energy is electric or silvery blue which cleanses worn out thoughts and conditions and promotes relaxation. The energy of

this center is associated with the communication of intuition, and when flowing freely, allows you to hear your inner voice guided from the creative force.

6. ***The Brow Chakra*** is located in your skull between your eyebrows. The color of its energy is indigo which promotes spiritual growth. The energy of this center, when flowing freely, joins the conscious with the innerconscious.

7. ***The Crown Chakra*** is located inside the top of your head. The color of its energy is violet which allows cosmic energy to flow in and out. The energy of this center is associated with the spiritual world, and when flowing freely, permits the mystic experience of enlightenment.

The collective purpose of all seven chakras is to absorb cosmic energy and distribute it evenly throughout the entire person. Each of the chakras, however, play a predominant role in this energy interflow in an ascending order from the purely physical to the purely spiritual.

The first and second chakras (the *Root Chakra* and the *Spleen Chakra*) function primarily to receive forces at a physical level through the human body: the energy from the earth and the vitality from the sun, respectively.

The third, fourth and fifth chakras (the *Solar Plexus Chakra*, the *Heart Chakra* and the *Throat Chakra*) function primarily to receive forces at a personal level or through the human soul: the lower astral energy from emotional intuition, the higher astral energy from clear intuition or intuitional love, and the lower innerconscious energy, respectively.

The sixth and seventh chakras (the *Brow Chakra* and the *Crown Chakra*) function primarily to receive forces at a spiritual level through the human spirit: the higher innerconscious energy from the union of the conscious with the innerconscious and pure cosmic energy from the total spiritual unfoldment, respectively.

With our knowledge and understanding of the function of the chakras, these swirling vortexes of auric energy, we can proceed to awaken them fully and achieve our maximum development of the body, soul and spirit. That is, we can achieve our natural ultimate condition of cosmic consciousness and vitality and total enlightenment and unfoldment. Your chakras may be awakened or developed to their fullest with the aid of three channels: (1) Appropriate nourishment through living food, (2) Appropriate breathing and bodily integration, and (3) Meditation. The chapters immediately following deal with these aids.

CHAPTER 6
MEDITATION

There is a general axiom in reference to meditation that states: the methods may differ, but the goal remains the same. There are also various motives for which people have employed the practice of meditation. In some traditions, meditation is used as a method for worship. In other traditions, meditation is used as a method to gain self-knowledge. In modern psychology, meditation is being used more and more as a therapeutic method. You yourself have been practicing meditation in your periods of deep relaxation and visualization and visioning. There is no mystery to meditation, and there is no difficulty in the practice of meditation. Meditation is as natural to the human as eating, sleeping, drinking or breathing. And one of the most important characteristics of meditation is that it is *effortless*.

Meditation simply is the discipline of looking inwardly. When we relax ourselves and suspend our attention from the distractions and complexities of the outside world and go inward, we then are able to know all levels of existence and the very center of consciousness itself. And that is the common goal of all meditation: to be still in order to tune into your innerconsciousness where you directly experience the One Consciousness or the Life Force Itself. In this state, all confusion dissolves, and your are in tune with the one Source of all being. That is, you are raised to the level of illumination and can know the how, why, what and where of everything, because your are in clear contact with the one Source of it all. The goal of all meditation is to experience this highest state of consciousness or the Superconscious Experience.

When we say that meditation is effortless, that is exactly what we mean. The practice of meditation requires no exertion, tension or force. On the contrary, using any effort at all will impede your inward journey to the inner world of your innerconsciousness. This is why it is helpful, at least when you are first beginning to incorporate the practice of meditation into your life, to have a quiet, dark space where you can be alone for your periods of meditation.

The more you experience the peace, joy and tranquil vitality in these periods of meditation where you are quiet and alone, the more you will find that you will be able to slip into the meditative state anytime during your normal daily activities. Eventually, your entire life will become a meditaiton, whether in your quiet periods of meditation or in your interaction with outside world, socializing, working and so forth. In fact your enjoyment and appreciation of these outside activities will become so dramatically increased because of your practice of meditation, that you will feel as though you never actually had experienced them really at all before.

A Simple Method of Meditation

Throughout my years of study and experience, I have found that *simplicity* is the key to everything, whether it be understanding a new concept, learning a new skill or practicing a new technique. This is especially true in meditation, since the very object in meditation is simplicity itself — that is, the One, Simple, Whole Source of all being. Complexity is fragmentary, and the one Source is not complex; It is whole. Also, the goal of meditation is to pierce through the scattered fragments and complexities around us and enter into the inner world to contact the one Life Force.

The following basic method of meditation will be thoroughly effective for centering your mind and transcending your complexities so that you may go inward to simplicity or the superconscious experience:

1. ***Decide to center your mind.*** Consciously decide that you are going to enter into an inner-conscious state of being where the only reality you will be aware of or centered on will be the one Reality or the Source of all being.

2. ***Go into the silence or deep relaxation.*** Here in relaxed, tranquil state of mind, allow your attention to be focussed or centered on the one object of your meditation. Allow your attention to be centered *only* on this one object, but *do not force* it. Just let this single-minded concentration flow effortlessly and naturally out of you to the object of your meditation. Keep going deeper and deeper into your inner consciousness.

3. ***Surrender your ego to higher consciousness.*** Scattered thoughts and sensations may start popping into your mind and body as you journey inward. This is because the more deeply

inward you go, the more acutely sensitive you become to the more subtle vibrations of existence. Do not let them distract you either by fighting them, *trying* to ignore them or involving yourself in them in any way. That is to say, do not extend any energy or effort to them, do not react to them. As you keep yourself centered on the object of your meditation with perfect ease, simply let these scattered thoughts and sensations rise to the surface and float away passively. They will dissipate of their own accord when you lend them no active attention or energy.

These entitites are merely "after-images", so to speak, of complexities that your ego or consciousness has been bombarded with all your life, and many of their traces have been imbedded in your subsconscious. During the process of meditation they tend to pop out all over the place. Let them go *passively*, and they will dissolve into nothingness, because they have no energy or existence of their own. Only you, your ego, can give them life through any kind of reaction to them, and this will cause your meditation to be interrupted. Just simply let them go by, let your ego relax and surrender it to your higher consciousness where you experience the Source of consciousness itself.

4. ***Enjoy the deluge of the superconscious experience.*** You may experience a sense of perfect peace, a sense of truly being *home*. You may experience omnipotence and omniscience — mainly, because in this inward state, you actually are at the source of all power and knowledge. You may experience a great, brilliant, all-consuming light that fills, illumines and magnifies your very being in such a fantastic way that no one ever actually has been able to put it into words. You may hear distinctly "unearthly voices" of guidance. There are countless forms of experiences which may accompany your contact with your inner Consciousness, and it may be different each time you go inward. But the one thing you most definitely *will* experience when you reach your inner Consciousness is the serenity of *knowing without confusion* and an *abiding peace and joy* that will carry over into your active life even when you are not in these quiet meditational periods.

The wonderful insight that you gain in meditation that carries over into your life is the inseparable Oneness of Life and the realization that we are one with this Eternal Reality and that we always were and will be part of its boundless and endless creative force. It is this true sense of well-being — of *real* being — that lets your absolutely know that you ARE, that you can DO anything, and that you can HAVE everything. This is why, that although the goal, or object of meditation is the Life Force Itself, we may employ meditation for any other specific needs or desires that we wish to manifest. We also may use meditation in conjunction with affirmation, visualization and visioning. In other words, meditation is a true state of being that can be used as an aid to the manifestation of our desires and our unfoldment.

Opening and Balancing the Chakras in Meditation

We can awaken the full energy of our chakras during our periods of meditation:

1. ***Go into meditation to the source of all being***. Feel the Universal Energy of the Life Force flooding your body and spirit. Surrender yourself to the super conscious experience and enjoy it for as long as you like.

2. ***Focus this energy on each chakra one by one***. Start with the root chakra and allow cosmic energy to pour into this center feeding and freeing the energy of this vortex to its

fullest. Feel it swirl and pulsate with ever-increasing speed and expansion. See the color of the chakra (in this case, fiery red) spinning more and more freely and growing greater, until it is finally flowing and glowing completely freely and easily. Continue this procedure with each chakra in their ascending order. Always keep focussing on the swirling motion of each chakra and on the color vibration of energy of each chakra. Feel each chakra giving and receiving energy to and from the others. By the time you have completed this procedure with the crown chakra, all of your chakras will be opened and balanced and flowing freely, and you will experience an incredible fullness of energy, vitality and balance, physically and spiritually. This is another method through which you can allign yourself with Universal Energy of the Life Force at will.

The Kundalini or Serpent-Fire

The seven schools of yoga in India (Raja Yoga, Karma Yoga, Jnana Yoga, Hatha Yoga, Laya Yoga, Bhakti Yoga and Mantra Yoga) all recognize the importance of the opening or developing of the chakras, as do all conscious-expanding techniques that have been cultivated more recently in the West. In fact, many of the western techniques for consciousness raising have drawn heavily from the more ancient traditions of the East.

The Indian school which deals most extensively with the seven chakras is Laya Yoga. Its method of opening the chakras is by arousing what is called the *Kundalini* or *Serpent-Fire* and forcing it through the chakras one by one. The kundalini is described as a force of fire in the form of a serpent which lies coiled dormant in the base of the spine in every person at the root chakra. It is a very powerful force of liquid fire that, when aroused, shoots upward in a coiling manner through the spine and chakras and finally pours out of the crown chakra. The kundalini is a very powerful force that affects a person on many levels, and its awakening should be approached with great understanding and care. When aroused properly in an evolved individual, it can awaken your full potential, physically, intellectually, astrally and spiritually. You may arouse the kundalini during meditation, but first be certain that you have proceeded far enough in your development when you do this. Because the force of the serpent-fire is so powerful, if it is aroused improperly or prematurely in your spiritual development, it could create real damage such as extreme physical pain, total disorientation, or even depravity as it passes through your chakras in an uncontrolled manner.

There have been instances when the kundalini has been aroused spontaneously without conscious attempt on the part of an individual, even in people who never even had heard of its existence. Very often in these cases, the person suddenly gained the faculty of clairvoyance which remained with them ever since, even after the overwhelming experience of the arousal of the kundilini passed when the kundalini settled back. It any event, just be sure that you have advanced in your development sufficiently in order to handle this experience before arousing the kundalini or serpent-fire within you. If you are not certain, it would be wise to consult someone who is trained in this area for guidance. You may inquire at any ashram or usually at any holistic center in your area.

Meditation always has been an essential aspect of the human experience, although the various methods of meditatation that have been developed throughout human history differ in their approach. The sufi or dervish in the Islam tradition meditates in the crowded city streets annihilating himself to the Divine Consciousness, while the Rishi in the Hindu tradition retreats to a cave or a place of solitude to join the Divine Presence. In the Christian tradition, meditation takes the form of meditative prayer or reflection on the Christ within which is the guide to God. In the Hasidic tradition of Judeism, meditation is the affirmation of the Harmony of the Divine in chanted phrases. Meditation in Jainism is an inside investigation, awareness and transformation with no ritual, no baptism, no ceremony. In Zen Buddhism, meditation is accomplished with the eyes partially open quietly looking at a blank wall, while in yoga, meditation is done with the eyes closed as the meditator concentrates on a particular word, thought or image. In the Tibetan method of meditation, the meditator centers attention on sounds, while in traditional Buddhistic meditation, the attention is centered on the breath. In transcendental meditation, the initiate is given a phrase called a "mantra" on which to center his attention, and so on.

But whether through sounds, breath, chants, prayers or dance, the object of all methods of meditation remains the same: to direct the consciousness inward where the Self may join the universal Self or the Life Force. Though usually the various methods of meditation that have been developed in human history are most compatible to the culture in which they have evolved, any method that proves efficacious to your entering into meditation will be appropriate for you. As we have said earlier, the simple method of meditation presented in this chapter will be thoroughly effective, but investigate other methods should you feel so inclined.

CHAPTER 7
LIVING FOOD NOURISHMENT

The key or vehicle to spiritual unfoldment and enlightenment at the biological level is the "light" body. The light body is one whose cells and tissues are thoroughly clear of wastes, toxins and dead material and thoroughly nourished with all the essential elements necessary for life. As you no doubt know, the cells of your body constantly are dying and being replaced with new cells. The old cells are meant to be expelled from the body through the four major channels of elimination: the lungs, the skin, the lymph and the colon. When you cleanse your body of dead material and rebuild and nourish it with living food, healthy living cells then replace the old ones in this process. This leads to health, longevity, vitality, energy and enthusiasm. Such a condition of bodily health and vitality naturally helps to free and ease the mind which, in turn, helps open and expand the inner Self to the Life Force. In fact, you may think of living food nourishment as a way of ingesting the Life Force on a biochemical basis.

The more you ingest life through living food nourishment, the more alive you become. On the other hand, the more devitalized material you take into your body, the more sluggish, dense and devitalized your body becomes. Aging and sickness is the result of improper elimination and improper nourishment. Disease, both biologically and spiritually, is brought about through poor elimination and the lack of living food nourishment. It is therefore important as we progress on our spiritual journey that we keep our bodies clean and fully alive, since the body and spirit are so intertwined with each other.

Elimination

Because most of us have not spent our entire lives eating only natural living food in a properly balanced combination, we have accumulated a certain amount of waste or dead material that is clogging many of our systems, especially the eliminative systems. If this dead material is allowed to build up for too long a time, toxemia is the result, disease sets in, and extreme, unrelieved toxemia results in death. Many people are walking around tired and listless unaware that this build up of dead material is taking place in their bodies, and they often do not take any corrective measures until at some point they are diagnosed as having a certain illness or condition. How much easier it is to rejuvenate your body *before* a serious condition takes hold and to live a life filled with energy, enthusiasm and enlightenment.

The colon or large intestine is possibly the most important organ of elimination as well as the last area of absorption in the alimentary canal or the digestive system. The colon also is, unfortunately, one of the more misunderstood and neglected parts of the human anatomy. Because the colon is a vehicle for both elimination and absorption, it is absolutely vital that it be kept clean and healthy. In addition, the colon is reflexive to *every other part of the body.* This means that the cleanliness — and, therefore, health — of *any* tissue of the body such as liver, kidney, brain, etc. depends upon the cleanliness and health of the colon. It has become evident in all my years of research and others' that virtually every disease has its origin in an unclean and unhealthy colon.

The colon, like every other part of our bodies, is kept healthy and balanced through natural living food nourishment or appropriate nutrition. But since most of us have ingested an abundance of devitalized, processed foods, a certain amount of sticky, hard, putrified, dead material has adhered layer upon layer to the mucous lining of the colon. Whether or not we have bowel movements every day or even several times a day, the old matter that has adhered to the colon wall is not moved, and the build up will continue as long as we continue to ingest devitalized foods that adhere to the colon wall. Many people are unaware that they are carrying around five to forty pounds or more of this poisonous, hard matter in their colons that slowly reabsorbs into the blood stream and lymph and leads to autointoxication and illness. In addition to the toxicity of this putrified matter, the weight of it causes pressure on the other organs in the body cavity, including the heart, and can interfere with their proper functioning even at a mechanical level. It is, therefore, once again necessary that we realize we must clean out our colons and rebuild our tissues with natural living nutrients.

Colonic Irrigation and Enemas

The obvious way to clean out encrusted, unwanted material inside a thing in the most gentle manner is by rinsing it out with water repeatedly until the object is clean. This is what is accomplished in the colon through colonic irrigation and enemas. For colonic irrigation, you go to a colonic therapist who rinses the dead matter from your colon for you. You may administer enemas to yourself at home.

Your colon is a large, flexible tube about five feet long which ascends from the end of your small intestine in the right side of your abdomen above the groin up to just below your rib cage on your right side. It then turns and crosses inside your abdomen under your stomach to your left side. At your left side just under your rib cage, the colon makes another turn and descends down your left side to your rectum and to your anus where the fecal matter ultimately is eliminated. The food that you take in through your mouth travels down your throat to your stomach through your small intestine and into your colon. Digestion begins through enzyme action in the saliva in your mouth. The food then travels to your stomach where further digestion takes place. The food then enters the small intestine, which is over twenty feet in length, where most of the nutrients are absorbed to nourish your body. The unassimilated and undigestible matter which is left then enters the colon where the final absorption takes place and through which the left over fecal wastes ultimately are eliminated from your body out of your anus. In severe cases of constipation, the colon is not able to eliminate at all. But even if a person is having "regular" bowel movements and is ingesting devitalized food which adheres to the wall of the colon, that person is not eliminating all of the fecal matter which is entering the colon each day. That person is constipated; that is, there is a certain amount of putrified, dead material impacted in the wall of the colon which is being slowly reabsorbed by the body and preventing the full vitality of the body, and this waste must be removed.

In colonic irrigation, the colonic therapist removes this waste by slowly letting in small amounts of water into the colon through a tube inserted into the anus. The therapist massages the colon gently to aid the release of the impacted material and lets the water containing the dead matter out. The therapist repeats this letting in of water, soaking and massaging the colon in small amounts and letting out the waste filled water for about an hour. You simply have only to lie there comfortably. By the end of the session, the colonic therapist usually has been able to remove a significant amount of old built up fecal matter from the entire colon(as well as, of course, the new feces that may be in the colon at that time). In the beginning, a series of colonic irrigations is most effective for cleaning the colon optimally, because some of the old matter stuck to the wall of the colon has been there for a number of years and may take a while to loosen completely and be expelled. To contact a colonic therapist for an appointment, you may check the yellow pages under colonic irrigation, chiropractic or physiotherapist or inquire at any holistic center in your area.

To administer an enema to yourself, simply go to a pharmacy and purchase an enema bag and a colon tube at least eighteen inches long. Remove the rectal syringe from the tube of the enema bag should it have one and attach the colon tube in its place. Fill the bag with tepid water and hang it on a door knob or a hook on your bathroom door. Lie down on your right side (preferably on a slant board, if you have one)., insert one-third of the colon tube into your colon through your anus gently and let one-third of the water in the bag to flow in. Clip off the water flow and gently massage the left side of your abdomen where your descending colon in located. Then, lie on your back and move the tube another third of the way into your colon, let in another third of the water from the bag, clip off the water flow and massage your transverse colon across your abdomen under your stomach. Finally, lie on your right side, insert the remaining third of the colon tube and let in the remaining water from the enema bag. Pull the tube out and massage your ascending colon in the right side of your abdomen. At this point, you may shake your pelvis as vigorously as you can, lift your legs straight up and move them is a bicycling motion or move your abdominal area in any way that feels appropriate to free the fecal matter for optimum release. Then allow the water and freed fecal matter to be expelled from your colon. This is done best in a squat position as it keeps the rectum from bending and allows the water and waste to flow with gravity. (At any time during this process, if you feel an urgent need to expel, pull out the tube and do so and then continue. Do not hold anything in when you feel the need to elimate.)

The irrigation of the colon or the washing of the colon is a procedure that has been practised by the human in all civilizations in recorded history and, no doubt, before. In recent times, in our culture, this very essential hygienic process seems to have been not only overlooked, but almost unheard of. With the new awakening that presently is occurring in all humans at this time on this earth, colonic hygience once again is being recognized and practiced by an ever growing number of individuals as a fundamental and essential aspect of health.

Living Food

Living food may defined broadly as any uncooked, organically grown vegetable, fruit, seed, grain, nut or sprout. Stricktly speaking, the spout is really the only *living* food, because it is actually alive — still growing — even after it is harvested, and even as you ingest it. All the other uncooked, organically grown foods are defined as living food as well, because they do not deplete the biochemistry of the body as they are digested and assimilated. On the contrary, they rebuild and rejuvenate the cells and tissues of the body and maintain and, if necessary, restore the body's biochemical balance. This simply means that they keep the body *alive* — to its fullest. In the perfectly healthy and balanced body, living food will maintain the full vigor and optimum functioning of the body. In the less than healthy or degenerate body, living food will restore the body to health. That is to say, living food will heal the body, or better, will allow the body to heal itself. This is because the body (like the mind or the spirit or any thing in Nature), given the opportunity, automatically will move toward improvement, health and perfection. At the cellular level, you can give your body this opportunity to be thoroughly alive and healthy through living food nourishment.'

Only uncooked, organically grown living foods contain the essential enzymes, vitamins, minerals, proteins, carbohydrates and fats necessary for the life of the human body in their natural state. When you nourish your body with living food, your body does not have to work to get the nutrition it requires from the food. The more your body has to work for the nutrients it needs to keep alive from the food you ingest, the more it is depleted of its own reserve of life-sustaining components. This is particularly true in the case of enzymes. Enzymes are proteinaceous substances produced by living cells that are essential to life, because they initiate and control all biological reactions in the organism such as cellular break down in digestion, temperature and energy control, hydrolysis and oxidation, etc.. At birth, your body has all the enzymes it needs, but should you persist in ingesting devitalized foods in which the enzyme content has been destroyed, your body gradually will be depleted of its own enzymes as it strives to derive nutrition from what you are ingesting.

Because living food has not been devitalized (through processing, cooking, drying, roasting, burning, freezing, chemicalizing, embalming or preserving), it contains its own enzymes and, therefore, does not exaust your body's supply of enzymes in the digestive process. In other words, in the digestion and assimilation of living food, the body is not drained, stressed or overworked to maintain its life. In fact, with living food nourishment, the body not only is (1) keeping alive, (2) maintaining its capacity to function, but also (3) is living in a state of progressive and positive good health. This is what we mean by nutrition.

You may purchase uncooked, organically grown living food at any organic food market or farm in your area. You may find it more expedient to grow your own living food in your house or apartment.

CHAPTER 8
BODILY INTEGRATION

Another approach or aid to spiritual harmony and balance is bodily harmony and balance. In addition to proper nutrition, the body can be balanced and opened and "lightened" through appropriate exercise and body work, including such techniques as stretching, breathing, yoga, massage and Structural Integration. Your spirit does not exist somewhere outside of you — and neither does your body. Yet it is surprising how many people are not in touch with their own bodies really at all. Too many people regard their bodies as solid, dense, fixed material objects that are somehow there to sit on, lie on, walk on and so forth, when in actuality, the body is a flexible, fluid field of energy that is in a process of constant change. The body is *not* solid or dense — it is a lithe and pliant projection of life, consciousness and energy. You are your body, and you are your spirit, and your body and spirit exist in an ever-moving and ever-changing interrelationship. It is because of this that bodily harmony is necessary for spiritual harmony and vice-versa.

Although the body is one entity, one unified whole, it is also a complexity of components, such as blood, bone, muscle, skin, connective tissue and so on that requires appropriate integration and balance in order to function ideally. When any part of the body is out of harmony with the rest, the whole system is thrown off, and when the system is out of harmony in itself, the body is thrown out of harmony with the eternal cosmos or Life Force of which it is a part. So, on a structural and "flesh" basis, it is important to keep the integration and balance of the body intact, released and flowing and in cosmic congruity. This can be accomplished both through certain exercise techniques which you can do on your own and through body work which is done with you by a trained body worker.

Exercise

What exercise does essentially in the body is to allow the structural parts of the body (such as muscle, bone, joints, etc.) to become and remain relaxed and limber and allow the bodily fluids (such as blood, lymph, etc.) to be oxiginated and to flow freely. There are a number of books on various forms of exercise including walking, running, aerobic exercise, swimming, dancing, stretching and breathing that you may investigate as you develop your own personal exercise program. There are also countless spas and clubs that offer exercise programs. Hatha yoga, which was developed in the ancient Hindu tradition of India, has become very popular in the West and is particularly beneficial for its emphasis on stretching, posturing, breathing and meditation. Any form of exercise (like anything else), of course, can become a meditation the more you tune into your body and your spirit as you proceed in your program and in your program and in your development. Research and experiment with as many exercise techniques as you like. Pursue whichever techniques that seem most suitable to you as you progress. But the important thing is to Do it — because change, which is growth or improvement, cannot take place without your allowing it to happen through active initiation and participation on your part. In order for the body, which is energy, to be fully alive, the energy must be allowed to flow freely; and movement, stretching, relaxation and breathing are vital aids to this process. The value of exercise cannot be emphasized too much.

Body Work

Body work is the manipulation of the tissues of the body by a body worker or practictioner. The fundamental function of body work (whether it be reflexology, chiropractic, polarity, shiastsu, massage Structural Integration etc.) is to balance the energy field of the body by freeing the constricted or blocked areas, and, thereby, allowing the whole body/energy to move into a more appropriate space. Moving into a more appropriate space allows a thing to progress positively toward its natural perfection. Body work gives your body this opportunity. All the many types of body work are extremely beneficial to this end and will effect significant progress and improvement for absolutely everyone. Possibly the two most fundamental — and indispensable — types of body work are massage and Structural Integration.

Massage

Massage is the manipulation of certain tissues of the body for remedial and hygienic purposes. It is accomplished by the rubbing, stroking, kneading or tapping of the entire body by a professional massage practioner. At the physical level, the emphasis of massage is with the muscular, circulatory and lymphatic systems. As the massage practioner systematically rubs or strokes your body, your muscles are relaxed and toned as your blood and lymph are moved and cleaned as they are permitted to flow more freely. Since the blood feeds and cleans all of the cells, tissues and systems of the body, it is obviously necessary that the blood itself be kept clean and flowing freely. Massage stimulates blood circulation and alleviates sluggishness in the circulatory system so that it may function easily. The debris which the blood picks up from all parts of your body as it exchanges oxygen and nutrients for the cellular waste products is dumped into your lymph in order to be eliminated. In most of us, our lymphatic systems can become even more sluggish and congested than our circulatory systems, so it is essential that we keep our lymph "awake" and moving fluently in order for the cellular wastes to be eliminated from our bodies. Massage accomplishes this as it manipulates and stimulates the natural flow of the lymphatic system, thereby allowing it to perform its function.

Another important purpose of massage is the release of tension. Tension, which we can experience very noticeably at the muscular level, is mostly — if not always — emotional and psychological in origin. Even if we do not feel tension, when we are not very in touch with our bodies, with ourselves, it may be existing within us subtly and even chronically. Such a condition causes restriction to our full functioning and a great, if subtle, drain on our vitality. When this tension is released through massage, a surge of heightened energy permeates our beings as we move into a state of released and increased vitality and well-being. This release, though produced by a physical, hands-on method, is not only physical in nature, but also emotional, psychological and spiritual. That is to say, though massage is bodily in its approach, it serves to liberate the mind and the spirit as well as the body. This is because massage, like all body work, deals in the release of energy, which in turn releases tension or stress, since the body is itself an energy field.

A very intrinsic, yet too often disregarded, aspect of the body that massage not only recognizes, but also works with tangibly, is the communicative force which permeates the entire body. Your body is expressing itself constantly, both within itself and in its relationship to the outer world. The more attune we become to our bodies, the more aware we become of what they are expressing about themselves and their relation with their environment, the world within them and the world outside with which they are connected. In other words, the more we tune into our bodies, the more we are in tune with *ourselves* and our interrelationship with all people, all things and the whole universe.

Massage helps us to become more finely and deeply aware of this bodily communicative force through the use of touch. Massage recognizes the fact that the sense of touch is as viable a contact with reality as is, for example, the sense of sight — and sometimes more direct. In fact, body energy can be experienced directly through touch, and the development of personal growth and unfoldment advanced and heightened by this experience. Massage is a tactual tool that allows us this experience of body energy in an ever-progressing manner with each session.

Structural Integration

Structural Integration (formally known as Rolfing) is a form of deep body work which deals with the manipulation of the connective tissue of the body for remedial structural purposes. It is accomplished by the application of pressure to the connective tissue by a professional Rolfer or Structural Integration practioner in an established order of systematic strokes. During a session, the Rolfer alternately uses hands, fingers, knuckles and elbows to contact your connective tissue. Connective tissue is a web of soft, flexible tissue that covers all of the muscles and joints of the body and supports the musculature and skeleton.

This soft, flexible connective tissue becomes dense and rigid due to improper movement or behavior patterns, trauma or injury, stress or tension, malnutrition and so forth. When the connective tissue becomes rigid or looses its flexibility, it restrains the normal movement of your muscles and joints and holds your skeleton in a restricted, contracted condition which keeps your body out of balance. In the process of Structural Integration, the connective tissue is freed and restored to its natural condition of flexibility. This return of flexibility to the connective tissue, in turn, releases the muscles which it holds which, in turn, release the skeleton. The structure, therefore is given more room or availability to move into a more appropriate space.

The purpose of Rolfing or Structural Integration is to establish balance in gravity: That is, to allow the body to move comfortably and naturally in balanced verticality in the gravitational field of the earth. When your structure is being held down or restrained, it is straining and working against gravity with every movement. When your structure is released and balanced, it moves *with* gravity — in fact, it is supported by gravity. Rolfing restores the natural balance to the structure of the body by restoring the body's natural flexibility, so that the body can move in ease and harmony within the earth's gravitational field.

Another significant effect Rolfing has on the body is to open it. Through the freeing of the structure, the whole body is freed. Other parts of the body, such as organs, blood vessels and nerves, are given more room to perform their functions more easily and freely. Your lungs, for example, will have more room to breathe to their full capacity, your heart will have more space to pump your blood more easily, your nerves will have more extension to convey their messages more precisely, and so forth. In other words, your body becomes more expansive and liberated at all levels through Structural Integration.

Although Rolfing was developed for bodily integration at the purely structural level, one of the most dramatic effects of this work takes place at the psychological level. As connective tissue returns to pliancy, thereby restoring the body to flexibility and balance, the mind also becomes balanced and supple.

CHAPTER 9
BODY, MIND AND SPIRIT

Our bodies can release our minds and our spirits, and our minds can release our bodies and our spirits, and our spirits can release our bodies and our minds. When your body is open, healthy and balanced, your mind and awareness becomes expanded, and your spirit is allowed to flow freely. So, too, when your mind or consciousness is expanded, your body becomes unrestricted, and your spirit unrestrained. And when your spirit, your Self, is set free, the energy field of your body alligns with Universal Energy, and your mind is alligned with Cosmic Consciousness.

The body, the mind and the spirit are interacting and interdependent systems within a person and expressions of the person. Personal health, perfection, joy and enlightenment are a result of the harmonious and total functioning of all three. When your body, mind and spirit are opened and balanced in their natural state of perfection and participation in the one Life Force, your full congruity is realized within the whole You and with the Whole Itself, the Life Force. It is in this state of Cosmic Consciousness — or, really, Existence — that anything can be actualized and everything can be experienced.

Many individuals (Plato, Bacon, Dante, Blake, Balzac, Emerson, etc.) who have reported the cosmic experience have reported that it occurred spontaneously and unexpectedly and, in most cases, just once in their lifetimes. It is, however, possible to allow this state of Awareness into your life at will on a regular basis through the use of certain disciplines or tools. It has been the purpose of this book to share those tools with you so that you may enter and remain in cosmic awareness — your natural existence — any time you like as long as you like.

As you increasingly understand the Natural laws and concepts unfolded in the preceeding chapters as you practice and employ the methods for your unfoldment and enlightenment, you will notice an every-quickening growth process in you. You will become more and more sensitive to the more subtle and the more tremendous vibrations of life. Absolutely everything in the universe can be experienced in a countless variety of vibrational levels from the most heightened to the most dismal. We are entirely free to choose the levels we wish to experience; and we, therefore, can choose the highest and best for ourselves. It takes nothing more than our awareness, expansion and love.

We all have the power to release or withdraw our awareness with our bodies, our minds and our spirits. The experience of limitation or of being controlled from the outside occurs only when we choose to make ourselves dense, when we contract ourselves and our awareness. I cannot reiterate enough that *all potential Experience and Fulfillment already are existing in you at this moment*. And you have the power to actualize any or all of it RIGHT NOW. You need only to *open*, to *unfold*, to *allow* yourself the expansion to pour it out of you and thereby receive it. When you choose to allow yourself this liberation by employing the methods for contacting and harmonizing with the Life Force, you will discover an old, forgotten simple truth: that you truly are unlimited. You will realize your inherent infinite power for Joy and Love and everything else in the Universe. You will experience and express the Center and Source of your Being and know that you can employ It to allow into your life *anything and everything you want.*

Possibly one of the most damaging statements or attitudes that has been going on far too long is "Nobody's perfect" or, "I'm not perfect, and neither are you". Nothing could be farther from the truth. The reality is that all of us are perfect — you are perfect, and so is everyone else. It is only that our Natural perfection has been clouded and inhibited by conditioned and habitual attitudes and belief in imperfection for ourselves and for others. This gives rise to ego deficiency which creates ego centricity or a feeling of isolation, because the ego, the consciousness, the mind has been restricted to the belief in imperfection or deficiency of the Self and the unlimited possiblity of the Self. Many aggressive and destructive self-defeating behavior patterns have resulted as a consequence of such an attitude, as well as unnecessary devitalizing depression and anxiety. The human, then, begins to feel like a victim of life who must struggle to keep afloat rather than an essential part of the flow of life and co-creator with the Life Force.

We are thoroughly free to think and act from a constricting place of fear and scarcity or from an unlimited space of Love and Abundance. When you choose to believe in fear and scarcity, your false belief will be proven true for you, because such a conviction will manifest fear and scarity in your life. (Remember, whatever you think, say or do, true or false, real or unreal, expansive or dense, will be manifested in your experience, in your life.) But when you release your body, mind and spirit of such inadequate and deficient belief systems and exist in and act from the *real* space of Love and Abundance, all the benefits of the Life Force will manifest in your life on all levels: physically and materially, mentally and emotionally, spiritually and transcendentally.

It is a natural ability in the human to transcend even the most restricting or demoralizing conditioning or programming at any instant and enter into our natural condition of Joy, Love and Prosperity. We are not molded or confined by our past — or even by our future. Our true Selves exist in an ever-present NOW where our potential, our power, is already complete, and we can call on it or join it any time we want. We are existing and intwined with all expressions of the Life Force, and all of Its great resources are at our behest. This immense Wealth and Power is within you and around you and for you awaiting your release, command and allowance, physically, mentally and spiritually. Relax and let It flow.

APPENDIX
AFFIRMATIONS
(SPIRITUAL MIND TREATMENTS)

The following are some examples, of Affirmations, which are known also as Spiritual Mind Treatments. The purpose of such treatments is to allign the mind or the consciousness with the Absolute or the One Life Force. That is, to change the attitude of the human mind from self-imposed illusory belief in restriction to awareness and knowledge of our true nature of Wholeness and Perfection. In this way, we can allow our lives and ourselves to be manifested to there fullest constantly and ever-increasingly. As we have said earlier, the success of the method of Affirmation depends upon the conviction you put into your affirmations. Do not, therefore, hope or merely believe, but *know* your endless Power and Opportunity as you treat your mind with your affirmations.

"I am One with the Totality of the Life Force. Total Love, total Happiness and total Prosperity fills me to overflowing and pours out of me and into me."

"I now release all the Love, Joy and Abundance of the Life Force within me, and I now receive Its limitless benefits into my life permanently."

"I am at peace and in perfect harmony with myself and the Universe. I love everybody, and everybody loves me."

"I now allow the power of the LIfe Force to flow freely through me. All seeming obstacles are disolved, and my way is clear, successful and easy."

"The Life Force within me now wipes out all doubt, fear, anger, resentment and anxiety, and infinite Love pours through me. This radiant magnetic current draws all perfection to me now."

"My boundless good flows to me in my life and affairs in a steady, uninterrupted ever-increasing stream of Happiness, Health and Abundance."

"My endless good now is lavished upon me in endless ways."

"I now let go of everything, and all the Abundance of the Life Force rushes to me. My perfection is complete and ever-growing."

"Nothing can oppose my good. I am surrounded with a brilliant White Light of protection, peace and positivity."

"I do not force the manifestation of my perfect Health, Wealth, Love, Joy and Self expression. I relax and allow all which has always been mine to spring to me now."

"I am guided by the direct inspiration of the Life Force, and I always follow my intuition instantly."

"I now let go of worn-out ideas and worn-out things and allow into my life everything I want — and more."

"I spend money freely knowing this increases my supply — any my supply is unlimited."

"I love freely, and boundless love is lavished on me."

"I give freely, and I receive freely and easily."

"My heart is open, and my mind expands and supports my intuitional guidance; and my life unfolds perfectly."

"I do not entreat — I *proclaim* my Oneness with absolute Good, absolute Health, absolute Love, absolute Joy, absolute Wisdom and absolute Prosperity."

"I do not expect — I *know* all the power of the Life Force is manifested in me now."

"I am the perfect cause manifesting the perfect effect."

"I am and express perfect Vitality, Health, Life, Activity, Enthusiasm, Abundance, Love and Joy. I am complete Freedom and Increase."

ABOUT ANN WIGMORE

As the founder of Hippocrates Health Institute, Ann Wigmore has dedicated her life to teaching others the value of living food. Born in Lithuania in 1909, she was raised by her grandmother, who gave her unwaivering confidence in the immense healing power of nature. Ann Wigmore spent years experimenting to find simple, healthy, and inexpensive ways to grow food indoors, such as the now popular technique of sprouting. Much of her philosophy is as old as Hippocrates himself who taught that if given the correct nourishment, the body will heal itself, and advised, *Let food be your medicine.*

In 1963, under her direction, the Hippocrates Health Institute became a philanthropic, non-sectarian, non-profit organization and study center implementing the principles of living food, wheatgrass chlorophyll, and care of the body for the restoration of vibrant health. Countless are those who have studied and healed themselves there, or who have profited from the knowledge of others who returned eager to teach and help.

In a desire to share her knowledge as broadly as possible, Ann Wigmore has authored over fifteen books, distributing over one million copies. She has lectured in twenty countries. Her ongoing healing work, with decades of experience backing it has given others a greater understanding and appreciation of the healer within.

If you have any questions about Ann Wigmore and her wholistic health program, feel free to write or call the Ann Wigmore Foundation at the following address:

Ann Wigmore Institute
P.O. Box 429
Rincon, PR 00677
(787) 868-6307 phone
(787) 868-2430 fax

Ann Wigmore Foundation
P.O. Box 140
Torreon, NM 87061
(505) 384-1017

INDEX